A CLOSE CALL

Anna Kenna

illustrated by David Elliot

NELSON
Language
ARTS

ɪ⓪ᴘ ⋅ International Thomson Publishing
The ITP logo is a trademark under licence.
www.thomson.com

Published 1999 by ɪ⓪ᴘ Nelson,
a division of Thomson Canada Limited,
1120 Birchmount Road,
Scarborough, Ontario M1K 5G4
www.nelson.com

First published 1999 by Learning Media Limited,
Box 3293, Wellington 6001, New Zealand

ISBN 0-17-618638-7

Printed in Hong Kong

9 8 7 6 5 4 3 2 1

Chapter 1

Harry dunked his spoon into his cereal and tried to sink the enemy ships. He pushed them down into the milky ocean, holding his spoon on top so that they couldn't bob back up.

"Harry, for goodness' sake, stop playing with your breakfast. Eat it!" said his mom.

Harry made a face, and his baby sister, Tiffany, giggled. She was squashing banana through her fingers and mixing it with a puddle of milk on her highchair tray.

As Harry spooned the last of his breakfast into his mouth, he watched his dad limp into the kitchen. He was wearing one sock.

"It's always the same," his father muttered, digging in the laundry basket. "I can never find a pair of socks."

Harry's mom went to the bedroom, opened the dresser drawer, and pulled out the missing sock. She dangled it in the air and waited for Harry's dad to take it. She winked at her son and smiled. "Dad's got a big day today. He's a bit uptight."

Harry knew that his dad had been up half the night working on some drawings for a shopping mall. He'd got really mad when Harry's rat, Barney, kept nibbling the edge of the drawings he'd laid out on the carpet.

"Yaaaah!" squealed Tiffany. She slapped her little hands into the sticky mess on the highchair tray.

"Come on, Harry," said Mom. "Move it, or you'll be late for school."

Harry brushed his teeth and then spent ten minutes trying to find Barney. He had to put him in his cage before he went to school. But his little rat friend was playing games. Harry couldn't find him anywhere. He went downstairs again just as his father was leaving.

"Bye, Harry!" his father yelled. "Have a good day at school."

"OK, Dad. See you later."

Harry sat down on the sofa to tie up his shoelaces.

That's when he saw it, poking out from under the armchair. Its one green eye was flashing. It was his father's cell phone.

Harry picked up the phone and turned it over in his hands. It felt really cool. He flipped it open and pushed one of the spongy buttons. It gave a loud beep. Harry jumped. He looked down the hall, but his mom was in the bedroom changing Tiffany. She hadn't heard.

"Harry, for goodness' sake, get going!" she yelled.

Harry knew that he should have told her about the phone, but he snapped it shut and slipped it into his knapsack. "Anyway," he thought, "Dad will be well on his way to work by now. I'll just look after it for the day."

"Bye, Mom," he called and ran out the door.

Chapter 2

The first call came as Harry was biking to school with his friend Sam. Sam stared at Harry's knapsack. "Hey, Harry, what's that noise?" he asked. "Your knapsack's ringing!"

Harry wobbled to a stop and fished the phone out of his knapsack. "Ah, hello," he said in his deepest voice.

"Ed," said a woman's voice. "Glad I caught you. Would it be OK if you used the visitor's parking space today? We've given your space to Charlotte Wu, the client you're meeting with this morning."

Sam had his ear pressed to the other side of the phone. His mouth was wide open.

"Yeah, fine," said Harry in a voice borrowed from his father.

"Great!" said the woman on the other end of the phone. "See you when you get to work."

Harry's dad was almost at work when he realized he'd left his cell phone at home. He was *not* pleased. He was having a bad day. First there was the missing sock; now the cell phone. Then, as he swung into the car park under his office building, he found that someone with a big silver car had taken his parking space.

He slammed the car door and threw his keys to the security man. "Get that silver tank towed away," he thundered.

Meanwhile, back at school, Harry's knapsack came to life again ... in the middle of math.

"Treep ... treep ... treep ... treep!"

Mr. Beazley swung around. His eyes narrowed as he looked around the classroom. Just as his thin lips were about to open, Sam began to cough, drowning out the phone. Harry moved quickly. "I need to be excused, please, Mr. Beazley," he said as he grabbed his knapsack and slipped out the door.

In the corridor, Harry flipped open the phone and half-whispered, "Hello."

"Sorry to bother you, Ed," said his mother's voice. "I just called to warn you that Barney might have crawled into your briefcase again. He's nowhere in the house."

"Hmm ... OK," said Harry in a gruff voice. He ended the call before his mother could say another word. He stood for a moment feeling rather ill. Then he threw the phone into his knapsack

and went back into class.

Chapter 3

Across town, on the sixth floor of
Flinders Architects, the meeting with
Charlotte Wu was going very well indeed.

"Well, Ed, I like it a lot," said Mrs. Wu,
running her fingers over the drawings.
"You've got yourself a job."

Ed Flinders relaxed for the first time in his difficult day and smiled as Charlotte Wu droned on about her plans for the new shopping mall.

"Anyway, we can talk about all that later," she said. "Let me buy you lunch. My car is parked right outside."

It was also lunch time at school. Harry had never been so popular. Everyone wanted to hold the cell phone. He'd let Reuben Polanski use the phone to order his lunch. In exchange for a ride on Marco Vanelli's new mountain bike, Harry had let him call his big brother who lived in another city.

Then some big kids got in on the act. Marty Millar snatched the phone off Harry. "Aw, cool, man," he said, pulling the aerial up and down.

"Wicked," said Luke Daley as he played his fingers over the beeping numbers. "But I don't reckon this is yours, Harry Carry."

Harry felt himself going bright red as the other boys now looked at him suspiciously. "Is so," he said. Just at that moment, Mr. Beazley came around the corner.

"Nice to see you big boys spending your lunch hour with the young ones ... how sweet," he said, rocking back and forth on his highly polished shoes. "Would someone like to tell me what's going on here?"

"Ah ... *nothing*, sir," said Luke Daley, who'd quickly put the phone behind his back.

Harry gulped as Mr. Beazley looked around the group. The boys hardly breathed as he stared at each of their faces.

Disappointed that he hadn't busted a playground scandal, he was just about to move off, when –

"Treep ... treep ... treep ... treep!"

Harry thought he was going to faint. Luke got such a fright that he threw the phone to Harry.

In a spectacular move, Mr. Beazley lunged forward and caught the ringing phone in his right hand. After pushing a few wrong buttons and saying "Hello … hello," he finally found the right one. "Ah, Mr. Flinders," he said in his most teacherish voice. "Beazley here. Yes, we met at the school last week."

Harry felt weak at the knees.

"Ah, ha … hmm, I see," said Mr. Beazley.

The older boys were leaning toward him, ears straining to hear.

"Well, no," said Mr. Beazley, "I must say that it wasn't a good idea, not even for a technology lesson. Still, no harm done. I'll keep it in my office for the rest of the day."

Chapter 4

"**I** think I've just saved my son from getting into trouble," said Ed Flinders as he sat down at the restaurant table. "I'll have to talk to him about this when I get home."

Charlotte Wu was in a better mood than she'd been in an hour ago, after she'd discovered her car missing.

"Kids," said Mrs. Wu, shaking her head. "I've got three of my own. You just wouldn't believe the mischief they get up to!"

After lunch, they relaxed over coffee and talked about the new mall.

"Can I see those drawings again?" said Mrs. Wu. "I'd like to check a couple of things."

Harry's father opened his briefcase and reached inside. His hand froze as it wrapped around a small, furry body.

Without thinking, he held the fat, white rat up in front of his face. Charlotte Wu sat frozen, holding a piece of chocolate cake just outside her open mouth. A group at a nearby table left in a clatter of cutlery and crockery. The waiter's eyes nearly popped out of his head.

Barney was not happy either. He didn't like the bright lights, and someone had picked him up in the middle of his lunch. He was still chewing and had bits of paper stuck in his teeth and whiskers. Barney had just eaten the first three pages of plans for the Meadowview Mall.

Chapter
5

After school, Harry's dad was parked outside, waiting for him.

"Ooh, Harry Carry, your dad looks mad," gloated Marty Millar. "I'm off!"

As Harry walked up to the car, the window slid down. "Get in," said his father.

Harry dropped his bike onto the grass and climbed into the car. He couldn't look at his father's face.

For what seemed like ages, his father said nothing. Then suddenly he blurted out, "I believe you have something that belongs to me, and I have something that belongs to you." He reached inside his briefcase and pulled out the sleepy rat.

Barney soon woke up when he saw Harry. He scampered up his arm and tickled his chin with his whiskers. Harry didn't smile.

"Harry, you have caused me no end of trouble today," his father began. "You had no right …"

The lecture went on for ages. Words like "honesty" and "respect" came up quite a bit. Harry tried hard not to cry. Sam Morrison was waiting for him behind a tree, and Harry thought he might see.

Harry felt really sorry for his dad as he heard about the important client's car being towed away and then Barney turning up at lunch.

"Is she still going to give you the job, Dad?" Harry asked in a shaky voice.

"I don't know," said his dad. "Barney wriggled out of my hand and was running around the restaurant. By the time I caught him and went back to the table, Mrs. Wu had gone."

At home that night, everybody was very quiet. Harry saw that his mom's and dad's faces were really serious at dinner. Even Tiffany ate her mashed vegetables instead of dropping them on the cat.

Later, when Harry was upstairs doing his homework, the phone rang. His dad seemed to talk to whoever it was for ages. Then he came into Harry's room, looking happier than he'd looked all night.

"Harry, someone would like to speak to you." Harry went downstairs and picked up the phone.

"My name's Charlotte Wu," said the voice on the other end.

Harry felt his cheeks going red, and he began to twist the phone cord around his fingers.

It was a pretty short conversation. Harry listened mostly, and then he said, "Yes, I know. Yes, he's the best … Thank you, Mrs. Wu. I'm really sorry about what happened." As he put down the phone, Harry heard his mom and dad scurry away from the bottom of the stairs, where they'd been listening. He followed them into the kitchen.

"I'm really glad Mrs. Wu's going to give you that big job after all, Dad," Harry said, looking at the floor, "and I really don't mind cleaning her car for the next six weeks, as long as I can borrow your car polish."

Harry was about to go upstairs again when he saw his dad's cell phone lying on the sideboard. He stopped, walked over slowly, and picked it up. He turned around, went back, and slapped it into his father's hand.

"And, Dad, *please* don't leave your stuff lying around," he smiled. "I'm getting really tired of tidying up after you."